Butterflies
by David Carter

Series editor: Roger Phillips

Elm Tree Books in association with the British Museum
(Natural History)

INTRODUCTION

Aim

In this book we have figured and described the habits of 84 species of European butterflies. These include all those known to occur in the British Isles and a number of other species that are likely to be encountered while on holiday in continental Europe.

How to use this book

As butterflies may be found at various times of year, according to the locality in which they are found, it is not possible to arrange them by season as in the plant volumes in this series. They are therefore arranged in their family groupings as shown below.

One photograph of each species shows the living butterfly in its natural habitat. The other photographs are of study specimens with their wings outspread to display their distinctive patterns. Both uppersides and undersides are shown and, in the many cases where males and females are considerably different from each other, both sexes are figured. These specimens have been specially selected from the world famous collections of the British Museum (Natural History) in London.

Why study butterflies?

The study of butterflies has been popular for at least two centuries, but interest has manifest itself in different ways over the years. The Victorian era marked the heyday of the collector, and butterfly collecting has remained popular until quite recent times. However, present day attitudes towards collecting have changed radically and, in most cases, the net has been replaced by a camera and butterfly watching is becoming a popular pastime.

Brimstone Butterflies

The reason for this change relates to an increasing awareness of the need to conserve our native wildlife. There is little doubt that our dwindling populations of butterflies are in need of protection. Although a few species are happily still common and even increasing their range, most have suffered serious decline in recent times and many are now endangered. Whilst it is unlikely that over-collecting has ever been directly responsible for the extinction of any species, pressures on our butterfly populations are so great today that any further depletion of stocks could tip the balance towards extinction.

The key to butterfly conservation is protection of their habitats and in order to do this we must understand the requirements of each species. If an area of countryside is rich in butterflies, it is a fair assumption that other forms of wildlife will also be flourishing. On the other hand, lack of butterflies may mean that an area has been damaged or disturbed in some way. Destruction of habitats is going on all around us and changes in the environment caused by various forms of land development, such as house and road building, and agricultural changes, such as the drainage of wetlands and the afforestation of moorland and mountain-sides, are having a profound effect on our butterflies.

Fortunately, they are very versatile and have managed to take advantage of newly created habitats resulting from man's activities. Parks and gardens provide a haven for many woodland and hedgerow species but other less obvious places, such as motorway verges and disused railway cuttings and embankments, also support a rich fauna of butterflies.

It is possible to attract butterflies to our own gardens by growing plants with nectar-rich flowers such as Buddleia (also known as Butterfly Bush), Sedum and Michaelmas Daisy. If space permits, a patch of nettles will provide food for the caterpillars of the Small Tortoiseshell and its relatives and an area of uncut grasses may encourage various meadow butterflies to lay their eggs.

Arrangement of Butterfly Families

Key to symbols used

♂	male	♀	female
vern.	spring form	*aest.*	summer form
△	underside		
○	circle of 1 cm diameter to indicate scale		

Swallowtail

Swallowtail

Papilio machaon is a large and distinctive butterfly, widely distributed in continental Europe but, in the British Isles, confined to the Norfolk Broads where it is protected by law. The British Swallowtail is a fenland dweller and is smaller and darker than the continental subspecies which is a much stronger flier, occurring in a wide range of habitats, particularly in flower-filled meadows and on sunny hillsides.

In many parts of Europe, this insect has two generations a year, with butterflies on the wing from April to August, although individuals only live for about three to four weeks. In Britain and parts of Northern Europe there is only one generation a year except in particularly warm summers.

Eggs are laid individually on the leaflets of Milk Parsley (*Peucedanum palustre*) or, in continental Europe, on Wild Carrot (*Daucus carota*) and Fennel (*Foeniculum vulgare*). The young caterpillars are black and white and resemble bird droppings but later become bright green, banded with black and spotted with red.

Swallowtail

Scarce Swallowtail

Scarce Swallowtail

Iphiclides podalirius is not as scarce as its vernacular name suggests although it is becoming less common in some areas and is protected in parts of central Europe. It is quite widely distributed in central and southern Europe but does not occur in the British Isles. It is most frequently found in orchards and lightly wooded areas but is a strong flier and may be seen on hilltops up to 1600 metres.

This species is easily distinguished from the Swallowtail by its longer tails, paler colour and the presence of six black bands on each forewing. There are two generations a year in the south, with butterflies on the wing from May to June and July to August, but north of the Alps there is a single brood, flying from May to July. Second brood butterflies are very pale and less strongly marked.

The caterpillars feed on the foliage of Hawthorn (*Crataegus*), Blackthorn (*Prunus spinosa*), Cherry (*Prunus cerasus*) and other cultivated fruit trees.

Scarce Swallowtail

Spanish Festoon

Spanish Festoon

Zerynthia rumina occurs in Spain, Portugal and south-eastern France. It is found on rough, stony, uncultivated slopes, particularly in coastal areas, and is one of the earliest butterflies to be seen on the wing. There is one generation a year, flying from February to May, depending on climate. The unusual, spiny caterpillars feed on the foliage of various kinds of Birthwort (*Aristolochia*).

Although the adult butterflies are very variable in patterning, they are distinguishable from the closely related Southern Festoon (*Zerynthia polyxena*) by the presence of distinct red patches on the upper surface of the forewings. The latter species occurs in south-eastern Europe, including south-eastern France, but is absent from Spain and Portugal. It is slightly later in appearance, occurring in April and May. It flies close to the ground and frequently settles on flowers and grass stems. Foodplants are the same as for the Spanish Festoon.

♂

♂ △

♀

♀ △

Spanish Festoon

Apollos mating

Apollo

Parnassius apollo is one of the largest and most distinctive of European butterflies. It occurs in mountainous regions of Europe, excluding the British Isles, but is becoming scarce in many areas. It lives mainly on mountain-sides, and in valleys and alpine meadows up to 2000 metres but in southern Scandinavia occurs in lowland habitats. Its slow fluttering and gliding flight makes it easy to capture and so it is particularly vulnerable to collectors. However, it is protected by law in many countries.

Butterflies are on the wing from June to September, according to altitude and latitude. The caterpillars feed on the fleshy leaves of stonecrop (*Sedum*) but are only active while the sun is shining, hiding under stones at other times.

Although this butterfly is extremely variable, with different forms occurring from one valley to the next, it can be distinguished from its rarer relative, the Small Apollo (*Parnassius phoebus*) by the absence of red spotting on the forewings.

Apollo

Large White feeding

Large White

Pieris brassicae is the common large 'Cabbage White' butterfly so frequently encountered in gardens and cultivated fields. It occurs throughout Europe, with the exception of northern Scandinavia. It is a highly mobile butterfly and, in the British Isles, the native population is reinforced by immigrants from continental Europe.

There are two or three generations a year and summer brood specimens are usually larger and more strongly marked than those occurring in spring and autumn. Butterflies are on the wing at various times from April to October.

The caterpillars are notorious pests of cabbages (*Brassica*) and related plants and are also found on garden Nasturtium (*Tropaeolum*). They sometimes completely skeletonise the leaves of entire crops. However, they frequently fall prey to grubs of a small parasitic *Apanteles* wasp. These live and feed within the host caterpillar, eventually emerging to spin a mass of small yellow cocoons alongside its body.

♂

♂ △

♀

♀ △

Large White

Small White feeding

Small White

Pieris rapae is the smaller of the two familiar 'Cabbage White' butterflies and is common and widespread throughout Europe, including the British Isles. Although this is primarily an inhabitant of gardens and other cultivated land, it also occurs along hedgerows and woodland margins.

Butterflies are on the wing from March to September with two generations a year in the north and three in the south. Spring brood individuals are much less strongly marked than those appearing in the summer. Like the Large White, populations in the British Isles are often reinforced by immigrants from continental Europe.

The caterpillars not only feed on cabbages (*Brassica*) and their relatives but also on various wild plants of the family *Cruciferae* as well as garden Nasturtium (*Tropaeolum*) and Mignonette (*Reseda*). When living on cabbages, the caterpillars bore into the hearts and feed inside so that damage to the crop is not noticed until it is too late. However this species is seldom as serious a pest as the Large White.

♂

♂ △

♀

♀ △

Small White

Green-veined White at rest

Green-veined White

Pieris napi is easily distinguished from the 'Cabbage Whites' by the presence of greyish green bands running along the veins on the underside of the hindwings. It occurs commonly throughout Europe, including the British Isles. Although it is frequently seen in parks and gardens, it prefers damp hedgerows, meadows and woodland margins.

There are one or two generations a year in the north and three in the south, with butterflies on the wing from March to October. In the British Isles they do not appear until late April or early May. This is a very variable species, ranging in colour from white to bright yellow and sometimes heavily suffused with grey. However the green veining is always distinct, although also variable in extent.

The caterpillars feed on Hedge Mustard (*Sisymbrium officinale*), Garlic Mustard (*Alliaria petiolata*), Lady's Smock (*Cardamine pratensis*) and other related wild plants.

16

♂

♂ △

♀

♀ △

Green-veined White

Black-veined Whites drinking at damp ground

Black-veined White

Aporia crataegi is the most distinctive of the white butterflies and occurs in many parts of Europe except for Scandinavia and the British Isles. It occurred quite commonly in parts of Britain in the mid-19th century but unaccountably went into decline and became extinct by 1915. Even in its continental European strongholds, where it was once a fruit-tree pest, populations can fluctuate considerably and the species is not as common as it was formerly.

This butterfly lives in orchards, along hedgerows and in open country-side and may often be seen flying over fields of clover and lucerne. It is also attracted to the sugary honey-dew secreted by bean aphids and will drink from damp patches on the ground. There is one generation a year and butterflies are on the wing from May to July.

The caterpillars live together in a communal web, coming out to feed on the foliage of Hawthorn (*Crataegus*), Blackthorn (*Prunus spinosa*), Cherry (*Prunus cerasus*) and related fruit trees.

Black-veined White

Bath White

Bath White

Pontia daplidice is a resident of southern Europe but regularly migrates to other parts of Europe. It is only a rare visitor to southern parts of the British Isles. There are conflicting explanations for the common English name of this butterfly. Some claim that it arises from an early capture of the species at Bath while others relate it to a famous 18th century embroidery of a butterfly made in that city.

This butterfly lives on rough uncultivated land, rich in wild flowers, and is also attracted to fields of Clover (*Trifolium*) and Lucerne (*Medicago sativa*). It has a rapid and erratic flight. There are two or three generations a year and butterflies can be seen from February to September.

The caterpillars feed on the foliage of Rockcress (*Arabis*), Mustard (*Sinapis alba*) and related plants. Recent chemical studies suggest that the Bath White is a group of two closely related and very similar species, although differences in their biology and distribution have yet to be discovered.

♂

♂ △

♀

♀ △

Bath White

Orange-tip

Orange-tip

Anthocharis cardamines is found throughout Europe, with the exception of Scotland and northern Scandinavia. It is a common inhabitant of hedgerows, woodland margins and damp meadowland rich in wild flowers. There is one generation a year, with butterflies flying from April to July according to locality, although they are most commonly encountered in the spring.

It is only the male that has distinctive orange tips to the forewings, females being marked with black. When at rest, they conceal these distinctive markings behind the hindwings which are patterned in such a way as to blend with the flower heads and foliage on which the butterflies settle. The bluish green caterpillars closely resemble the seedpods of Lady's Smock (*Cardamine pratensis*), Garlic Mustard (*Alliaria petiolata*) and related plants on which they feed.

The closely related Gruner's Orange-tip (*Anthocharis gruneri*), which occurs in Greece and Yugoslavia, can be distinguished by its smaller size.

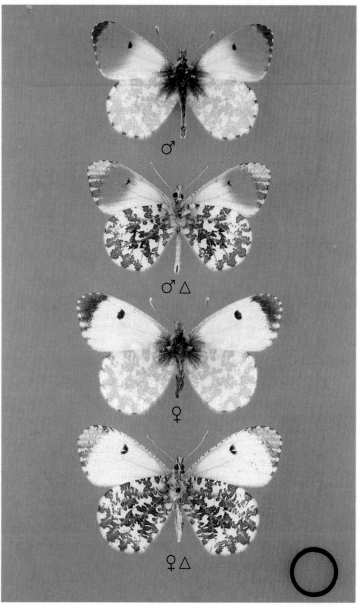

♂

♂ △

♀

♀ △

Orange-tip

Clouded Yellow at rest

Clouded Yellow

Colias croceus has a strong flight, enabling it to migrate to most parts of Europe from its breeding strongholds in Mediterranean countries. This butterfly cannot survive the winter in northern Europe but fresh migrants arrive in spring of each year and produce a further generation in summer or autumn. Although not always a common visitor to the British Isles, it sometimes arrives in large numbers along the south coast of England. In southern Europe, there is a succession of generations and butterflies are on the wing from April to September. These butterflies are quite variable and the female has a common form (*helice*) in which the ground colour is white. A number of similar but less common species occur in southern Europe.

The Clouded Yellow lives in open countryside and downland rich in wild flowers and is strongly attracted to fields of Lucerne (*Medicago*) and Clover (*Trifolium*) on which its caterpillars feed. Other foodplants are Birdsfoot Trefoil (*Lotus corniculatus*) and various vetches (*Vicia*).

24

♂

♂

♀

♀

Clouded Yellow

Female Berger's Clouded Yellow at rest

Pale Clouded Yellow

Colias hyale is another migrant with its breeding headquarters in southern Europe. It moves northwards into central Europe and occasionally occurs in some numbers along the North Sea coasts of Holland and Germany. It is a rare visitor to the south coast of England.

Migrant butterflies produce a second generation in summer but in southern Europe there is a third brood. They are on the wing from May to September and can be seen flying over fields and downland, particularly in chalk and limestone regions. The caterpillars are green with a red-marked white stripe along the sides. They feed on Clover (*Trifolium*) and Lucerne (*Medicago*).

Berger's Clouded Yellow (*Colias australis*) is so similar to the previous species that it is almost impossible to distinguish as an adult. It is usually brighter in colour with a more prominent orange spot on the hindwing. However, the caterpillars are quite distinct, with yellow stripes and black spots, and feed on Horseshoe Vetch (*Hippocrepis comosa*).

26

♂

♂ △

♀

♀ △

Pale Clouded Yellow

Male Brimstone at rest

Brimstone

Gonepteryx rhamni is one of the first butterflies to be seen in the spring. It is widely distributed throughout Europe, with the exception of Scotland and northern Scandinavia. An old English name for this species is said to be the Butter-coloured Fly and probably provides the origin of the term Butterfly.

There is only one generation a year but individual butterflies may live for up to ten months. After emerging in summer they go into hibernation in the autumn, resting among the leaves of evergreen plants such as ivy, where they are very well camouflaged. They become active again early in the following spring, when they mate and lay eggs. They may be seen flying in gardens, along hedgerows and woodland margins and in open countryside, often far from their foodplants.

The caterpillars feed on Purging Buckthorn (*Rhamnus catharticus*) in chalk and limestone areas and on Alder Buckthorn (*Frangula alnus*) in wet and acidic regions.

28

♂

♂ △

♀

♀ △

Brimstone

Male Cleopatra feeding

Cleopatra

Gonepteryx cleopatra is a southern European butterfly found in Spain, Portugal, southern France, Italy, Greece and Yugoslavia. It lives mainly on scrubland and lightly wooded mountain slopes but also occurs in lowland meadows.

These butterflies have a single generation each year and, like the Brimstone, they overwinter as adults. They are on the wing from February to June and again from August to September, according to locality, and are strong and rapid fliers. This species is less widespread than the Brimstone but can be quite common in suitable areas. Males are easily distinguished from those of the latter species by the deep orange flush on the forewings. Females are less easy to recognise as they only show faint traces of orange on the underside.

The caterpillars feed on various species of Buckthorn (*Rhamnus*).

♂

♂ △

♀

♀ △

Cleopatra

Wood White feeding, northern Greece

Wood White

Leptidea sinapis is the smallest and most delicate of the white butterflies. It occurs locally throughout Europe, except Holland and parts of Scandinavia but, in the British Isles, is confined to a few localities in southern parts of England, Wales and Ireland. As its name implies, it lives in woodland clearings and the margins of forests, although it can also be found on wooded undercliffs and in old railway cuttings.

There are two or more generations a year according to locality and butterflies are on the wing in spring and summer. Their flight is very weak and they often flutter close to the ground. The caterpillars feed on Birdsfoot Trefoil (*Lotus corniculatus*), Meadow Vetchling (*Lathyrus pratensis*) and many other plants of the pea family.

The closely related Eastern Wood White (*Leptidea duponcheli*), occurs in southern Europe but can be recognised by the yellowish tint of the wings. The larger Fenton's Wood White (*Leptidea morsei*) is confined to Austria, Hungary, Rumania and Yugoslavia.

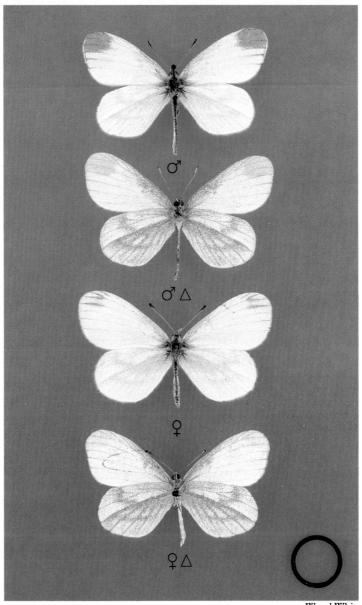

♂

♂ △

♀

♀ △

Wood White

Male Purple Hairstreak

Purple Hairstreak

Quercusia quercus is found throughout Europe with the exception of northern Scandinavia. It occurs in many parts of the British Isles, except for northern Scotland but is very scarce in Ireland. It usually lives in oak woods, although a single isolated oak tree can support a colony of these beautiful little butterflies.

There is one generation a year and butterflies are on the wing from July to September. Because they usually fly high in the tree tops, they are seldom seen, except when they come down to feed on the honeydew secreted by aphids. The caterpillars feed on young foliage of oak (*Quercus*).

The purple sheen on the wings of these butterflies distinguishes them from all other European species, with the exception of the Spanish Purple Hairstreak (*Laeosopis roboris*). However, the latter species, which occurs in the Iberian Peninsula and south-eastern France, has a purplish blue sheen with broad black borders and lacks the characteristic little tails on the hindwings.

34

♂

♂ △

♀

♀ △

Purple Hairstreak

Brown Hairstreak at rest

Brown Hairstreak

Thecla betulae is a butterfly of retiring habits and is seldom seen, even though it is widespread in Europe, ranging from southern Scandinavia to northern Italy. In the British Isles it is rather scarce and local, occurring in parts of southern England, Wales and western Ireland. This is the only European hairstreak to have a bright orange-yellow underside to the wings. It is primarily a woodland insect but also lives in well-established hedgerows.

There is one generation a year and butterflies may be found from July to early October, according to locality. Every year the butterflies of each colony congregate around a tall tree of their own choosing to perform their mating flight. Like many other hairstreaks, they generally remain high up in the tree tops, although they sometimes descend to feed at Bramble (*Rubus*) blossom. Their flight is rapid and erratic.

The caterpillars feed on the foliage of Blackthorn (*Prunus spinosa*), plum (*Prunus domestica*) and related plants.

♂

♂ △

♀

♀ △

Brown Hairstreak

White-letter Hairstreak at rest

White-letter Hairstreak
Strymonidia w-album is widespread in Europe but absent from northern Scandinavia and southern parts of the Iberian Peninsula. In the British Isles it is confined to southern England and Wales. The name of this butterfly refers to a white, w-shaped marking on the underside of the hindwing, which distinguishes it from all other European hairstreaks. It is one of the most elusive species, due to its retiring habits, living in woodland rides and along forest margins and hedgerows where elms grow.

There is one generation a year, with butterflies on the wing from June to August, according to locality. They tend to remain high in the tree tops but sometimes descend to feed at the flowers of Bramble (*Rubus*), Privet (*Ligustrum*) and other hedgerow plants.

The caterpillars feed on the foliage and flowers of Wych Elm (*Ulmus glabra*) and other species of Elm. Unfortunately, the devastation caused to their foodplants by Dutch Elm disease may have a serious long term effect on populations of this butterfly.

38

♂

♂ △

♀

♀ △

White-letter Hairstreak

Black Hairstreak at rest

Black Hairstreak

Strymonidia pruni is a widespread but local butterfly in central and eastern Europe. In the British Isles, it is the rarest of the hairstreaks, only occurring in the east midlands of England. Its vernacular name is somewhat misleading as it is much less black than its commoner relative, the White-letter Hairstreak. However it can be easily distinguished from the latter species by the presence of orange borders on the hindwings. It lives in woodlands and dense hedgerows where blackthorn thickets are established.

There is one generation a year and butterflies are on the wing in June and July. Although they generally remain in the tree tops, these butterflies may sometimes be seen feeding on aphid honeydew or at the blossoms of hedgerow shrubs such as Bramble (*Rubus*) and Privet (*Ligustrum*).

The caterpillars feed on buds and developing leaves of Blackthorn (*Prunus spinosa*) and related plants.

40

Black Hairstreak

Green Hairstreak on bramble

Green Hairstreak
Callophrys rubi is the commonest and most widespread of the hairstreaks, occurring throughout Europe, including the British Isles. The only similar species, Chapman's Green Hairstreak (*Callophrys avis*), is confined to the Iberian Peninsula and southern France and can be recognised by the reddish brown colouring of the front of the head.

The Green Hairstreak lives in habitats ranging from hedgerows and open woodland to downland and moors. It has one generation a year and butterflies may be seen from March to July according to locality. They make short, rapid flights low down amongst the branches of trees and shrubs and can be seen settling on vegetation, although the green colouring of the underside of the wings makes them quite difficult to detect. The males adopt their own territories and perch in prominent positions to await passing females. The caterpillars feed on the flowers and foliage of a wide range of plants, including Bilberry (*Vaccinium myrtillus*), various species of Furze (*Ulex*) and Buckthorn (*Rhamnus*).

♂

♂ △

♀

♀ △

Green Hairstreak

Small Copper feeding

Small Copper

Lycaena phlaeas is widespread and common throughout Europe, including
the British Isles. It lives in various rough, flowery grassland habitats,
including meadows, roadside verges, railway embankments, disused
quarries, downland, dunes and sea cliffs. Although there are several other
European butterflies of similar size with copper-coloured wings, none is
likely to be confused with this beautiful and distinctive species.

There are from two to four generations a year, according to climate and
locality and butterflies may be on the wing at any time from May to
October. However, in the far north there is an arctic subspecies that has
only one brood a year and flies in June and July. They are very active little
butterflies and are fond of basking in the sun with their wings outspread.

The caterpillars feed on the foliage of Common Sorrel (*Rumex acetosa*),
Sheep's Sorrel (*Rumex acetosella*) and related plants.

♂

♂ △

♀

♀ △

Small Copper

Large Copper

Large Copper

Lycaena dispar is one of the largest European butterflies of the family
Lycaenidae. It is quite widely distributed in central and southern Europe,
excluding the Iberian Peninsula, but only occurs in scattered and isolated
colonies. It became extinct in the British Isles in the mid-19th century but
examples of a similar Dutch subspecies were introduced to Wood Walton
Fen in 1927 and a breeding colony still survives there under careful
management. This species lives exclusively in wetland habitats such as
marshes and fens and is consequently greatly threatened by drainage of the
surrounding countryside for agricultural purposes.

Some subspecies of this butterfly are single brooded and on the wing in
June and July, while others have two broods and fly from May to June and
August to September. They have a rapid flight and are fond of basking in
the sun while resting on low-growing vegetation.

The caterpillars feed on the foliage of Great Water Dock (*Rumex
hydrolapathum*) and Scottish Water Dock (*Rumex aquaticus*).

46

♂

♂ △

♀

♀ △

Large Copper

Long-tailed Blue feeding

Long-tailed Blue

Lampides boeticus is widely distributed in tropical and subtropical regions of the world, ranging from the Pacific Islands to Africa, where it is sometimes a pest of plants of the pea family. In Europe, its main breeding grounds are in the south but butterflies migrate northwards each year, reaching as far as Holland and Germany. It is a rare visitor to the British Isles but is sometimes recorded from southern parts of England.

This strong-flying butterfly lives in a wide range of habitats but is most frequently encountered in rough, uncultivated places rich in wild flowers and in fields of Lucerne (*Medicago*). There are two or three generations a year and, in southern Europe, butterflies are on the wing from May to September. Migrants do not normally reach as far north as England until summer or autumn.

The caterpillars feed within the seedpods of Bladder Senna (*Colutea*), Everlasting Pea (*Lathyrus latifolius*) and related plants.

48

♂

♂ △

♀

♀ △

Long-tailed Blue

Male Short-tailed Blue

Short-tailed Blue

Everes argiades is fairly widely distributed in central and southern Europe, although it is absent from central and southern Spain. There is some migration to more northern parts of Europe and specimens occasionally occur in the British Isles. The first recorded English capture was on Bloxworth Heath, Dorset in the latter part of the 19th century and for this reason it is sometimes known as the Bloxworth Blue.

The habitats of this butterfly are damp flowery meadows, heaths and hillsides up to an altitude of 1000 metres. There are two or more generations a year and butterflies are on the wing from April to September. Males of the second brood tend to be a darker blue.

The caterpillars feed on the seeds and foliage of Medick (*Medicago*), Birdsfoot Trefoil (*Lotus corniculatus*) and related plants.

The Eastern Short-tailed Blue (*Everes decoloratus*) and the Provencal Short-tailed Blue (*Everes alcetas*) both lack the characteristic, strong orange spot near the tail on the underside of the hindwing.

♂

♂ △

♀

♀ △

Short-tailed Blue

Small Blue

Small Blue

Cupido minimus, sometimes also known as the Little Blue, is widespread and common in many parts of Europe, although it is absent from southern parts of the Iberian Peninsula and northern Scandinavia. In the British Isles it is widely distributed but generally rather scarce, except for a few places in southern Wales and England where it is still locally common. The closely related Carswell's Little Blue (*Cupido carswelli*), which lives in Spain, has purplish scales near the wing bases.

The Small Blue lives in small colonies in sheltered places on dry downland, cliffs and embankments, particularly in chalk and limestone districts. It often thrives in abandoned quarries and lime pits.

There are one or two generations a year and butterflies are on the wing from April to September. They are not very active and only make short flights, so they are easily overlooked.

The caterpillars live within the flowerheads of Kidney Vetch (*Anthyllis vulneraria*), feeding on the developing seeds.

♂

♂ △

♀

♀ △

Small Blue

Female Holly Blue

Holly Blue

Celastrina argiolus is one of the most distinctive of European blue butter-flies and is unlikely to be confused with any other species. It is widely distributed throughout Europe with the exception of northern Scandinavia. In the British Isles it is widespread, ranging as far north as south-western Scotland, but is most common in southern and central England. It lives in woodland clearings, hedgerows, parks and gardens.

There are two generations a year and butterflies are on the wing from April to May and again from July to August. They may be seen flying around hedges and ivy-strewn walls but are seldom attracted to flowers, preferring to feed on carrion or the sap from wounded trees. Second brood females often have the distinctive black borders to the wings more strongly developed.

The caterpillars feed on the flowers, berries and young foliage of various shrubs but particularly on Holly (*Ilex*) in the spring and Ivy (*Hedera*) in the autumn.

54

♂

♂ △

♀

♀ △

Holly Blue

Female Large Blue feeding

Large Blue

Maculinea arion is widely distributed in central and southern Europe, except for southern regions of the Iberian Peninsula. It is feared to have become extinct in the British Isles as no butterflies have been sighted there since 1979. It lives on heaths, grassland and hills, often in coastal areas.

There is only one generation a year and butterflies are on the wing in June and July. They are attracted to various wild flowers, including Wild Thyme (*Thymus serpyllum*) on which they lay their eggs.

This species has a remarkable life history as the caterpillars feed at first on Thyme but are soon picked up by ants which are attracted by the sweet secretions from 'honey glands' on their backs. The caterpillars are carried back to the ants' nest where they complete their development, feeding on young ant larvae.

This species can be distinguished from the Scarce Large Blue (*Maculinea telejus*) and Dusky Large Blue (*Maculinea nausithous*) by the presence of a bluish suffusion on the underside of the hindwings.

♂

♂ △

♀

♀ △

Large Blue

Female Silver-studded Blue, northern Greece

Silver-studded Blue

Plebejus argus is widespread throughout Europe, with the exception of northern Scandinavia. In the British Isles it is very local in occurrence and is largely confined to southern and eastern England and a few places in Wales. Its common name refers to the jewel-like silver spots on the underside of the hindwing. Although its most usual habitats are sandy heathlands, it also lives on dunes, chalk downlands and limestone cliffs.

There are one or two generations a year according to locality and climate and butterflies are on the wing from May to August. They are fairly active in fine weather, making frequent short flights amongst the heather but on dull days may roost together in large numbers on gorse and bramble bushes.

The caterpillars feed on the young tender foliage of various heathers (*Calluna and Erica*), Gorse (*Ulex*), Broom (*Cytisus*) and Birdsfoot Trefoil (*Lotus corniculatus*). Those belonging to a small local race living on coastal limestone in Wales feed on Rock Rose (*Helianthemum*).

♂

♂ △

♀

♀ △

Silver-studded Blue

Male Idas Blue, Italy

Idas Blue

Lycaeides idas is widely distributed throughout Europe, although it does not occur in some of the Mediterranean islands and is absent from the British Isles. It is so similar to the closely related but slightly larger Reverdin's Blue (*Lycaeides argyromemnon*) that it is sometimes very difficult to distinguish without examination of internal structures. It is also rather similar to the Silver-studded Blue but can usually be recognised by the narrower black borders to the wings of the male. There are many named subspecies of this variable butterfly, based on small differences in size and pattern.

Habitats are dry sandy heaths, hillsides and other rough ground, from lowlands up to an altitude of 1200 metres in the Alps. There is one generation a year in northern regions and two in the south.

The caterpillars feed on various plants of the pea family and have an interesting association with ants, which transport them to their nests where they overwinter.

♂

♂ △

♀

♀ △

Idas Blue

Northern Brown Argus, Scottish Borders

Brown Argus

Aricia agestis is one of the commonest and most widely distributed of
European butterflies, absent only from northern Scandinavia and Scot-
land. It lives on chalk grasslands, heathlands and coastal dunes and cliffs.
There are two or three generations a year, with butterflies on the wing from
April to August, according to locality.

The caterpillars feed on Rock Rose (*Helianthemum*), Stork's Bill (*Ero-
dium*) and Cranesbill (*Geranium*).

Northern Brown Argus or **Mountain Argus**, *Aricia artaxerxes*, occurs
in Scandinavia, Spain and parts of central and south-eastern Europe. In
the British Isles, it replaces the Brown Argus in Scotland and northern
England. It can usually be distinguished from the latter species by the
presence of a white spot in the centre of the forewing and by a lack of black
spotting on the underside. It lives in mountain and moorland habitats and
is on the wing in a single generation from June to August according to
locality. The caterpillars feed on Rock Rose.

Top: Brown Argus   Bottom: Northern Brown Argus

Male Mazarine Blue, southern Dolomites

Mazarine Blue

Cyaniris semiargus is widespread and common throughout continental Europe, with the exception of northern Scandinavia. It became extinct as a breeding butterfly in the British Isles in the late 19th century and now only occurs there as a rare migrant. It lives in rough uncultivated fields, rich with wild flowers, and alpine meadows up to 1800 metres. The violet-blue colouring of the male, combined with the small black spots on the undersides of the wings, distinguishes this species from all other European blue butterflies.

There is one generation a year, with butterflies on the wing from June to August according to climate and altitude. They fly low over the ground with a rather slow wingbeat and are fond of drinking from puddles and patches of damp earth.

The caterpillars feed on the flowers, seeds and foliage of Kidney Vetch (*Anthyllis vulneraria*), Clovers (*Trifolium*) and other related plants.

♂

♂ △

♀

♀ △

Mazarine Blue

Male Chalk-hill Blue

Chalk-hill Blue

Lysandra coridon is a distinctive species, occurring in most regions of Europe but absent from Scandinavia, Portugal and southern Spain. In the British Isles, it is confined to southern parts of England. It lives on downland and in meadows on chalk and limestone soils. Favourite haunts are south-facing grassy slopes and abandoned chalk pits. In suitable localities, it may occur in great numbers, but unfortunately this is one of the species that has been adversely affected by modern agriculture and populations have declined in some areas.

There is only one generation a year and butterflies are on the wing from July to September according to climate and locality. They are very active in sunny weather and have a strong and rapid flight but in dull weather they rest, head downwards, on grass stems.

The caterpillars feed on Horseshoe Vetch (*Hippocrepis comosa*). Like many related species, they secrete a sugary substance from 'honey glands' on their backs and are attended by ants.

♂

♂ △

♀

♀ △

Chalk-hill Blue

Male Adonis Blue

Adonis Blue

Lysandra bellargus is, as its name suggests, one of our most beautiful butterflies. It is widely distributed throughout Europe, with the exception of Scandinavia. In the British Isles it is restricted to a few localities in southern England. It lives on downland and other grassland on calcareous soils, often in the company of the Chalk-hill Blue, with which it sometimes hybridises. However, it is much more local in occurrence than the latter species. Males are frequently mistaken for those of the Common Blue but can be distinguished by their vibrant turquoise-blue colour and by black bands that extend across the white wing-fringes to produce an almost chequered effect.

There are two generations a year and butterflies are on the wing from May to July and August to September. Behaviour is similar to that of the Chalk-hill Blue.

The caterpillars feed on the foliage of Horseshoe Vetch (*Hippocrepis comosa*) and are frequently attended by ants.

♂

♂ △

♀

♀ △

Adonis Blue

Male Common Blue

Common Blue

Polyommatus icarus is one of the most common and widespread of European butterflies, ranging from the Mediterranean coast to the Arctic. It is widely distributed throughout the British Isles. Much of its success is due to the wide range of places that it is able to inhabit, from lowland meadows to grassy mountain-sides up to 2000 metres. Preferred habitats are downland, heaths, damp meadows, parks and gardens.

The number of generations varies from one a year in the north to three in the south and butterflies may be on the wing at any time from April to September, according to locality and climate. They are very active in sunny weather, making rapid but short flights amongst flowers and other low vegetation. In dull weather they rest, head down, on the stems and flower-heads of grasses.

The caterpillars feed on the flowers and leaves of Birdsfoot Trefoil (*Lotus corniculatus*), Rest Harrow (*Ononis spinosa*), Medick (*Medicago*), Clovers (*Trifolium*) and other plants of the pea family.

♂

♂ △

♀

♀ △

Common Blue

Duke of Burgundy feeding

Duke of Burgundy Fritillary

Hamearis lucina is widespread in central and southern Europe, with the exception of southern Spain. In Scandinavia, it is restricted to southern Sweden and to Zealand in Denmark while in the British Isles it is mainly confined to scattered localities in southern England. This species does not belong to the same family as the other fritillaries, but is superficially similar to them in appearance, even though it is more closely related to the blues and coppers. It lives in forest clearings, open woodland and scrub-covered downland, usually in lowland areas, although in some parts of Europe it occurs up to 1300 metres.

There is one generation a year in the north and two in the south with butterflies on the wing from May to August, according to locality. Males perch openly on the vegetation, waiting to pursue passing females. They have a rapid, buzzing flight.

The caterpillars feed on the foliage of Cowslip (*Primula veris*) and Primrose (*Primula vulgaris*).

♂

♂ △

♀

♀ △

Duke of Burgundy Fritillary

Nettle-tree Butterfly feeding

Nettle-tree Butterfly

Libythea celtis is most common in Mediterranean areas of Europe but occurs as far north as the southern slopes of the Alps. It is a very distinctive species with unusually toothed forewings and a prominent snout on the head that has given rise to the alternative name Beak Butterfly. It lives in lightly wooded areas, usually below 500 metres, although in late summer individuals may be seen at much higher altitudes.

There is only one generation a year. Butterflies emerge from the pupa in June and are active until September but then go into hibernation. In the following March and April, they re-emerge to mate and lay eggs. When at rest, with folded wings, they bear a remarkable resemblance to dead leaves.

The caterpillars feed on the foliage of Nettle-tree (*Celtis australis*).

Nettle-tree Butterfly

Two-tailed Pasha feeding on rotten fruit

Two-tailed Pasha

Charaxes jasius is largely confined to the Mediterranean coast of Europe. It is the only European representative of a large group of butterflies occurring in Africa. Dry hillsides appear to be the favoured habitat but these large and handsome butterflies are seldom encountered at altitudes above 800 metres.

There are two generations a year with butterflies on the wing from May to June and August to September. The second generation is often more abundant. Males are more active than females and have a powerful sailing flight. They usually rest high in the tree-tops but are sometimes seen when they descend to feed on rotting fruit.

The large and spectacular green caterpillars have four red-tipped prongs on the head. They feed on the foliage of the Strawberry Tree (*Arbutus unedo*).

Two-tailed Pasha

Male Purple Emperor

Purple Emperor
Apatura iris is one of the most handsome European butterflies, widely distributed in central regions but absent from the south-west and from Scandinavia. In the British Isles it is confined to a few areas of central and southern England. It is a woodland butterfly, mainly of lowlands but also up to 1000 metres in some parts of continental Europe.

There is one generation a year and butterflies are on the wing in July and August. The males have a strong, soaring flight and usually remain high in the treetops, frequently patrolling around a prominent oak (*Quercus*), where they can be found by the less active females. Although they feed mainly on aphid honeydew on the foliage of trees, they sometimes descend to feed on carrion or dung on the forest floor, particularly in woodland rides and clearings. This is the only time that they are normally noticed, otherwise they are seldom seen.

The caterpillars feed on the foliage of various Sallows (*Salix*).

♂

♂ △

♀

♀ △

Purple Emperor

Lesser Purple Emperor   Lesser Purple Emperor drinking on damp ground

Apatura ilia has a slightly more southern distribution than that of the preceding species, although it is also absent from the extreme south west. It does not occur in the British Isles. There are two colour forms, one in which the pattern is suffused with yellowish brown and the other very similar to the Purple Emperor. It can be distinguished from the latter species by the presence of a reddish orange-ringed, black spot on the forewing. As its name suggests, it is usually slightly smaller, although there is an overlap in size.

Its habitats and behaviour are very similar to those of the Purple Emperor but, although it is single brooded in northern parts of its range, there are two generations a year in the south. Butterflies are on the wing from May to June and August to September, preferring damp places, particularly by the sides of streams where the foodplants grow.

The caterpillars feed on the foliage of Poplar and Aspen (*Populus*), Willow and Sallow (*Salix*).

♂

♂ △

♀

♀ △

○

Lesser Purple Emperor

Poplar Admiral, southern Dolomites

Poplar Admiral

Limenitis populi is widely distributed in central Europe but it is local in occurrence and rare at the limits of its range. It is absent from the British Isles, northern Scandinavia and many parts of southern Europe. Males and females are quite similar in appearance but females are more extensively marked and banded with white. Apart from its larger size, this species can easily be distinguished from the White Admirals by the presence of a band of orange-red lunules on the hindwing. The usual habitats of this butterfly are deciduous and mixed woodlands, particularly forest clearings and along streams where the foodplants grow.

There is one generation a year and butterflies are on the wing from June to August, according to locality. They normally remain high in the treetops but may be seen in the mornings when they often descend to drink from damp muddy ground or to feed on dung and decaying carrion.

The caterpillars feed on the foliage of Aspen and Poplar (*Populus*).

Poplar Admiral

White Admirals feeding

White Admiral

Limenitis camilla is widely distributed in central Europe but only occurs in southern parts of Scandinavia. In the British Isles it is confined to central and southern England and a restricted area of south-eastern Wales. In southern Europe it is replaced by the closely related Southern White Admiral (*Limenitis reducta*) although in many parts of central Europe the two species occur together. The White Admiral can be recognised by the presence of a double row of black dots on the underside of the hindwing. It lives in deciduous and mixed forests, showing a preference for shady, damp situations.

There is one generation a year with butterflies on the wing from June to August according to locality and climate. They fly strongly in the treetops but are more usually seen when they descend to feed at bramble blossom along woodland rides.

The caterpillars feed on the foliage of Honeysuckle (*Lonicera*), choosing rather spindly plants that scramble amongst the branches of trees.

♂

♂ △

♀

♀ △

White Admiral

Large Tortoiseshell, southern France

Large Tortoiseshell

Nymphalis polychloros is widely distributed in central and southern Europe but becomes more scarce further north and is absent from many parts of Scandinavia. In the British Isles it was once quite widespread but has declined rapidly in the last forty years and is probably now extinct here as a breeding species. Rare recent sightings are most probably of migrants. It lives on the margins of woodland and along wooded lanes.

There is only one generation a year and butterflies are on the wing from June or July to September before going into hibernation, sheltering in such places as hollow tree trunks. They re-emerge in the following spring and may be seen from March to May, when they mate and lay eggs. In the spring they feed at Sallow (*Salix*) blossom, but usually they fly high in the treetops and are seldom seen.

The caterpillars usually feed on the foliage of Elm (*Ulmus*) but are sometimes also found on Willow (*Salix*), Poplar (*Populus*) and fruit trees.

Large Tortoiseshell

Camberwell Beauty feeding on over-ripe blackberries

Camberwell Beauty
Nymphalis antiopa is a distinctive, strong-flying migrant, occurring throughout Europe except for southern Spain and the Mediterranean Islands. It also occurs in North America, where it is known as the Mourning Cloak. It is a scarce visitor to the British Isles, the first recorded English specimen found in 1748 in Camberwell, London, giving rise to its common name. It lives in open and lightly wooded countryside but has a preference for the banks of rivers and streams where the caterpillars' foodplants grow.

There is one generation a year with butterflies on the wing from June to September, when they go into hibernation. They become active again in the following spring and may be seen from March to May or June, according to climate and altitude. They often feed on sap oozing from wounds in trees and are also attracted to over-ripe fruit.

The caterpillars feed on the foliage of Willow and Sallow (*Salix*).

Camberwell Beauty

Peacock on bramble

Peacock

Inachis io is the most distinctive of our common European butterflies, occurring almost everywhere with the exception of northern Scandinavia. In the British Isles it is widespread and common but becomes more scarce towards the north and is absent from many parts of Scotland. It lives in a wide range of habitats but shows a preference for wooded areas and is often found in parks and gardens.

There is one generation a year and butterflies are on the wing from July to October. They fly actively in sunny weather, feeding on flowers of thistles (*Carduus*), bramble (*Rubus*) and such garden plants as *Buddleia*. In late autumn they go into hibernation, hiding away in hollow tree trunks and in unheated outbuildings. If disturbed at this stage, they rustle their wings together to produce a snake-like hissing sound. In the following spring they become active again in order to mate and lay their eggs.

The caterpillars feed on the foliage of Stinging Nettle (*Urtica dioica*).

Peacock

Red Admiral on garden *Sedum*

Red Admiral
Vanessa atalanta is a common migrant species with its European breeding headquarters in the Mediterranean region. Each year it moves northwards into all other parts of central and northern Europe with the exception of the extreme north of Scandinavia. It is a regular migrant to the British Isles where this handsome species was once quite appropriately known as the Red Admirable. It lives in a wide range of habitats but seems most attracted to wooded countryside, orchards, parks and gardens.

There are two or three generations a year according to locality. Migrant butterflies usually produce further generations on arrival at their destination, although in areas such as the British Isles these may not survive the winter. Butterflies may be seen at almost any time between March and November. They have a strong and rapid flight and are attracted to a wide range of nectar-bearing flowers and to rotting fruit on which they feed.

The caterpillars feed on the foliage of Stinging Nettle (*Urtica dioica*).

Red Admiral

Painted Lady feeding

Painted Lady
Cynthia cardui is a migrant butterfly with its breeding headquarters in North Africa and southern Europe. Each year it moves north into most parts of Europe. It is a regular visitor to the British Isles, usually arriving in June, and is often seen in parks and gardens.

There are two or three generations a year according to habitat and climate. Migrant butterflies usually produce a further generation on arrival but in northern regions these seldom survive the winter. They are on the wing from April to October and have a rapid and powerful flight.

The caterpillars feed on the foliage of Thistles (*Carduus* and *Cirsium*) and on other plants such as Mallow (*Malva*) and Burdock (*Arctium*).

The closely related American Painted Lady (*Cynthia virginiensis*) is a rare migrant to various parts of Europe from North America. It can be distinguished from the Painted Lady by its smaller size and the presence of a row of blue eye-spots on the hindwing.

Painted Lady

Small Tortoiseshell on Buddleia

Small Tortoiseshell

Aglais urticae is probably the most common colourful European Butterfly, occurring throughout the Continent. In the British Isles it is widely distributed and often abundant. It lives in a wide range of habitats but its favourite haunts are the margins of fields, flowery roadside verges, waste ground, parks and gardens.

In most regions there are two generations a year but in the extreme north there may be only one. The first brood is usually on the wing in early summer and produces a second generation that emerges in late summer or early autumn and feeds actively for several weeks before going into hibernation. This takes place in almost any sheltered place, often in sheds, outhouses and other unheated buildings. These butterflies re-emerge in the following spring to mate and lay eggs. They are frequently seen feeding on both wild and cultivated flowers or basking in the sun.

The caterpillars feed on the foliage of Stinging Nettle (*Urtica dioica*), preferring clumps of young foliage in sheltered, sunny positions.

96

Small Tortoiseshell

Comma feeding, northern Greece

Comma

Polygonia c-album occurs throughout Europe with the exception of northern Scandinavia. In the British Isles it is widely distributed and common in central and southern England and in lowland Wales but absent from Scotland and Ireland. The populations of this species fluctuate in Britain and seventy years ago it was considered to be quite a rarity. It lives in woodland, hedgerows, parks and gardens and was at one time a feature of hop-growing areas. A distinctive white marking on the underside of the hindwing gives rise to both its scientific and common names.

The Comma has two generations a year. First brood butterflies are on the wing in early summer and are paler in colour and markings than the second brood that appears in late August or September and hibernates before mating and laying eggs in the following spring. When at rest with their wings folded, these butterflies resemble dead leaves.

The caterpillars feed on the foliage of Nettles (*Urtica*), Hop (*Humulus lupulus*) and Elm (*Ulmus*).

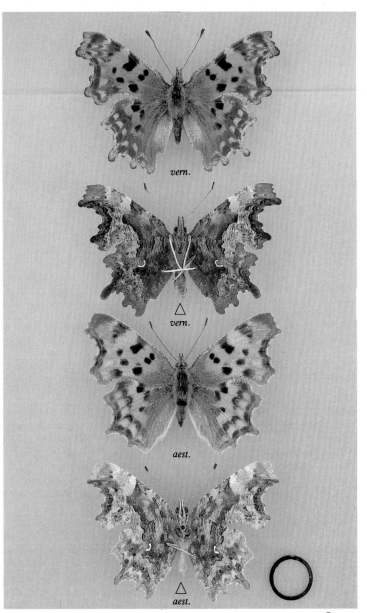

vern.

△ *vern.*

aest.

△ *aest.*

Comma

Map Butterfly feeding

Map Butterfly

Araschnia levana is widespread and common in central Europe but absent from Italy, southern France and Scandinavia. It does not occur naturally in the British Isles although colonies were introduced and established in Herefordshire and Monmouth at the beginning of this century. Despite their initial success, they were wiped out by collectors who disagreed with the introduction of 'foreign' species. The Map lives in open woodland and forest rides and clearings, generally in lowland areas and seldom above 1000 metres.

The interesting feature of the two annual broods is that they are quite different in appearance. The spring generation, on the wing in May and June is bright orange-brown with blackish markings while summer butterflies, flying in August and September, are predominantly dark brown with yellowish white bands. Unlike any other European butterfly, the female suspends its eggs in long chains from the foliage of the caterpillar's foodplant. The caterpillars feed on Stinging Nettle (*Urtica dioica*).

♂
vern.

♀
vern.

♂
aest.

♂ △

Map

Silver-washed Fritillary feeding, northern Italy

Silver-washed Fritillary

Argynnis paphia is a beautiful species, occurring throughout Europe, with the exception of northern Scandinavia. In the British Isles it is quite widely distributed but of local occurrence and absent altogether from Scotland and northern England. The characteristic silvery bands on the underside of the hindwings give this species its common name and distinguish it from any other European fritillary. A dark greyish brown form *valesina* occurs in some regions. It is a woodland species, usually seen in forest rides and clearings but sometimes also found in nearby hedgerows.

There is only one generation a year and butterflies are on the wing from June till September according to locality and climate. They are strong fliers, living high in the treetops but descending to feed at the flowers of Bramble (*Rubus*) and other nectar-bearing blossoms. The females do not lay their eggs on the caterpillars' foodplant but on nearby tree-trunks.

The caterpillars feed on the leaves of Dog Violet (*Viola riviniana*) and related species.

♂

♂ △

♀

♀ △

Silver-washed Fritillary

Dark Green Fritillary

Dark Green Fritillary

Argynnis aglaja is widely distributed throughout Europe except for the extreme north of Scandinavia. It is widespread in the British Isles, particularly in coastal regions, and is represented by a particularly handsome dark race in the western islands of Scotland. The common name of this species stems from the beautiful dark greenish suffusion to the underside of the hindwings. Unlike many other fritillaries, it is less common in woodland than in its other habitats, such as open downland and moorland, dunes and sea cliffs.

There is only one generation a year and butterflies are on the wing from June to August, according to locality and climate. They have a powerful and rapid flight, enabling them to move about freely in windswept country, but can often be seen feeding at the flowers of Thistle (*Carduus*) and other nectar-bearing plants.

The caterpillars feed on the foliage of various species of Violet (*Viola*).

Dark Green Fritillary

High Brown Fritillary drinking from damp ground, southern Dolomites

High Brown Fritillary

Argynnis adippe has a similar distribution to the previous species but its range does not extend so far north in Scandinavia. Thirty years ago, it was quite widely distributed in England and Wales but now it is much rarer and is only found in a few localities in Wales and western England. It is absent from Scotland and Ireland. This butterfly is easily confused with the Dark Green Fritillary but can be distinguished by the presence of an outer band of reddish-ringed silvery spots on the underside of the hind-wing. Its usual habitats are open woodland, woodland margins, scrubby hillsides and alpine meadows up to 1600 metres.

There is a single generation each year and butterflies are on the wing in June and July. They have a strong, soaring flight among the treetops but often descend to feed on the flowers of such plants as Thistle (*Carduus*) and Bramble (*Rubus*).

The caterpillars feed on the foliage of Dog Violet (*Viola riviniana*) and related species.

♂

♂ △

♀

♀ △

High Brown Fritillary

Queen of Spain Fritillary, northern Italy

Queen of Spain Fritillary

Issoria lathonia has its headquarters in Mediterranean countries of Europe and North Africa but regularly migrates northwards as far as southern Scandinavia. It is a rare visitor to the British Isles although one or two sightings are reported each year, usually from the south-east of England. This is one of the most distinctive and beautiful of the fritillaries with its characteristic forewing shape and large silver spots on the underside of the hindwing. It lives in rough open countryside such as heathland, and dry hillsides, occurring up to 2500 metres in mountainous regions.

There are usually two or three generations a year but, in the north, sometimes only a single brood. Butterflies are on the wing from March to October in the extreme south but migrants usually arrive in central and northern Europe in May and produce a second brood in late summer. Their flight is strong and rapid.

The caterpillars feed on the foliage of various species of Violet (*Viola*).

Queen of Spain Fritillary

Small Pearl-bordered Fritillary, northern Italy

Small Pearl-bordered Fritillary

Clossiana selene is widely distributed throughout Europe except for the
Mediterranean Islands, Greece and southern parts of the Iberian Peninsula
and Italy. In the British Isles it is still the most commonly encountered
small fritillary, occurring in many parts of Scotland, Wales and western
England, but has declined steadily in many English localities and is now
virtually absent from the midlands and the east. It is not recorded from
Ireland. Although primarily a woodland insect, preferring damp situations, this species also lives on heaths, moorland and hillsides up to an
altitude of about 2000 metres.

There is one generation a year in the north and two in the south, with
butterflies on the wing from April to August according to locality and
climate. In sunny weather the males fly actively low down amongst the
herbage, feeding on nectar-bearing flowers and seeking the less active
females. The caterpillars feed on leaves of Dog Violet (*Viola riviniana*) and
related species.

♂

♂ △

♀

♀ △

Small Pearl-bordered Fritillary

Pearl-bordered Fritillary feeding, southern France

Pearl-bordered Fritillary

Clossiana euphrosyne is more widely distributed in continental Europe than the previous species, occurring almost everywhere except for the south of Spain. In the British Isles, the situation is reversed and this species is less widespread. In the last thirty years it has declined seriously in many English localities in the east and midlands. The two species are very similar in appearance and habit and often fly together. The Pearl-bordered can be distinguished by the rather dull, yellowish-orange ground colour of the underside of the hindwing, contrasting in appearance with the brighter silver and reddish brown pattern of the Small Pearl-bordered. Despite their names, there is little difference in size.

There is one generation a year in the north and two in the south with butterflies on the wing from April to August depending on locality. They fly around quite rapidly low down in woodland clearings.

The caterpillars feed on the foliage of Dog Violet (*Viola riviniana*) and related species.

♂

♂ △

♀

♀ △

Pearl-bordered Fritillary

Glanville Fritillary

Glanville Fritillary
Melitaea cinxia is widespread throughout Europe with the exception of
southern Spain and northern Scandinavia. In the British Isles, however, it
is very local in occurrence and is only found on the Isle of Wight and the
Channel Islands. It lives on undercliffs, by roadsides and on rough
uncultivated slopes, particularly where the ground is rather unstable and
liable to disturbance. This attractive little butterfly was named after Mrs
Eleanor Glanville, an 18th century butterfly collector.

There is only one generation a year in the north but in southern Europe a
second brood occurs. Butterflies can be found from May to June and
August to September, according to locality. They fly low over the ground
and feed at various nectar-bearing flowers. The caterpillars feed communally on the foliage of Ribwort Plantain (*Plantago lanceolata*).

The similar but rather larger Freyer's Fritillary (*Melitaea arduinna*),
occurs only locally in parts of south-eastern Europe.

♂

♂ △

♀

♀ △

Glanville Fritillary

Spotted Fritillary, northern Greece

Spotted Fritillary

Melitaea didyma is a common and widespread species in many parts of
Europe, although it does not occur in Belgium, Holland, Scandinavia or
the British Isles. It is one of the most variable European butterflies, both
individually and geographically. No two specimens look quite the same
and there are several named subspecies. It is difficult to find a constant
feature by which this species can be recognised with certainty but the
underside of the hindwing usually has a distinctive line of round black
spots in the pale yellow marginal band.

The habitats of this butterfly are meadows, open woodland, scrubby
heathland and hillsides up to 1700 metres. There are two to three
generations a year with butterflies on the wing at various times between
May and August according to climate and altitude. They fly over flowery
slopes in warm, sunny situations.

The caterpillars feed on Plantain (*Plantago*), Toadflax (*Linaria*), Speed-
well (*Veronica*) and various other plants.

116

♂

♂ △

♀

♀ △

Spotted Fritillary

Heath Fritillary feeding, southern France

Heath Fritillary

Mellicta athalia is an extremely variable species, found in most parts of Europe, with the exception of Corsica and Sardinia. It is often quite difficult to distinguish from other continental species such as the False Heath Fritillary (*Mellicta diamina*), although the black-edged, yellow lunules on the underside of the forewing are characteristic.

In the British Isles, it is the rarest fritillary, confined to a few localities in south-western and south-eastern England, and is protected by law. Despite its name, this butterfly is often found in open or coppiced woodland as well as on heaths and meadowland and, in Scandinavia, on moorland.

There is one generation a year in the north and two in the south, with butterflies on the wing from May to September. Males patrol in woodland clearings in search of the less active females.

The caterpillars feed communally on the leaves of Cow-wheat (*Melampyrum pratense*), Ribwort Plantain (*Plantago lanceolata*), Foxglove (*Digitalis*) and other herbaceous plants.

118

♂

♂ △

♀

♀ △

Heath Fritillary

Marsh Fritillary

Marsh Fritillary
Eurodryas aurinia is a very variable species, occurring locally throughout most of Europe with the exception of Norway and the Mediterranean Islands. In the British Isles it is mainly confined to scattered colonies in western England, Wales and Scotland although it is more generally distributed in Ireland. As its name suggests, this butterfly is mainly found in wetland habitats, such as marshes and boggy fields, but also occurs on chalk downland and dry mountain-sides up to 1500 metres. In many areas populations have declined or become extinct due to land drainage.

There is only one generation a year and butterflies are on the wing from May to June. They fly low down amongst the vegetation but are generally rather sluggish. The caterpillars feed communally on the foliage of Devil's Bit Scabious (*Succisa pratensis*) and various species of Plantain (*Plantago*).

The closely related Spanish Fritillary (*Eurodryas desfontainii*) has distinctive black spots on the underside of the forewing.

♂

♂ △

♀

♀ △

Marsh Fritillary

Marbled White feeding, northern Italy

Marbled White

Melanargia galathea is widespread in Europe but does not occur in Scandinavia. It is the most common and widespread member of a distinctive group of similar species largely confined to southern and south-eastern Europe. Its most distinctive feature is a broken grey band on the underside of the hindwing, bearing a series of small, blackish eye-spots. In the British Isles it is largely confined to southern and south-western England and is absent from Scotland and Ireland. It lives in rough grassland, particularly on chalk downland and sea cliffs, and along the margins of woodland.

There is only one generation a year and butterflies are on the wing from June to September according to locality and climate. They have a rather slow, flapping flight and seldom stray far from their own colony. On warm, sunny days they can be seen basking or drinking nectar from the flowers of Knapweeds (*Centaurea*) and Thistles (*Carduus*).

The caterpillars feed on various grasses such as Fescues (*Festuca*).

♂

♂ △

♀

♀ △

Marbled White

Woodland Grayling at rest, northern Italy

Woodland Grayling

Hipparchia fagi is found in central and southern Europe, with the exception of central and southern Spain and Portugal. It does not occur in northern Europe or the British Isles. As its name implies, it is a woodland insect, found mainly in grassy clearings in lowland regions but also occurring at altitudes of up to 1000 metres.

There is only one generation a year and butterflies are on the wing from June until August. They are well camouflaged when they rest on the bark of tree trunks with their wings folded but will fly off if disturbed.

The caterpillars feed on various soft grasses but particularly on species of *Holcus*.

The very similar but smaller Rock Grayling (*Hipparchia alcyone*) generally lives in more open country up to altitudes of about 1800 metres and its distribution extends further north. However, where the two species fly together they can easily be confused.

Woodland Grayling

Grayling on heather flowers

Common Grayling

Hipparchia semele is widespread throughout Europe, with the exception of northern Scandinavia. In the British Isles, it is widely distributed but local, occurring mostly in coastal districts. It lives in dry grassland habitats such as heaths, downland and sand dunes, both on acid and calcareous soils. There are many named local races and subspecies and in southern Europe there is likely to be some confusion with the Southern Grayling (*Hipparchia aristaeus*) and Delattin's Grayling (*H. delattini*).

There is only one generation a year and butterflies are on the wing from May to August according to locality. They have a strong, rapid flight but often settle on the ground, usually selecting stony, sun-baked situations. When at rest, they tilt their wings to one side to reduce the shadow that they cast. This device, together with the well-camouflaged underside pattern, makes them very difficult to detect.

The caterpillars feed on various fine grasses, such as Sheep's Fescue (*Festuca ovina*) and Bents (*Agrostis*).

♂

♂ △

♀

♀ △

Common Grayling

Male Mountain Ringlet

Mountain Ringlet

Erebia epiphron is widely distributed in mountainous areas of Europe, with the exception of Scandinavia. In the British Isles it is restricted to parts of highland Scotland and a few mountainous localities in the English Lake District. There is considerable geographic variation and many subspecies are recognised. In continental Europe there are a number of similar species of *Erebia* but, by comparison, *epiphron* is rather dull in colour, usually with small black eye spots on both sides of the wings. It is a high altitude species, occurring on wet grassy slopes, often close to streams, up to 2000 metres.

There is only one generation a year with butterflies on the wing from June to August, according to locality and altitude. They only fly when the sun is shining, dropping down amongst the grass tufts as soon as the sun goes in. They have a slow, fluttering flight, low over the ground.

The caterpillars feed on Mat Grass (*Nardus stricta*) and similar species.

♂

♂ △

♀

♀ △

Mountain Ringlet

Female Scotch Argus on bramble flowers

Scotch Argus

Erebia aethiops is widely distributed in central and south-eastern Europe but absent from Scandinavia, the Pyrenees and the Iberian and Italian peninsulas. In the British Isles it is mainly found in the highlands and islands of Scotland, while in northern England it is confined to a few localities in the Lake District. It lives on boggy grassland in or near open woodland and on moors and grassy mountain-sides up to 2000 metres. In continental Europe, it can be distinguished from several other similar *Erebia* species by the presence on the underside of the hindwing of a pale grey band marked with a series of minute white dots.

There is only one generation a year and butterflies are on the wing from July to September according to locality. Like many other mountain species, they only fly when the sun is shining. The flight is relatively slow and low down amongst the vegetation.

The caterpillars feed on various grasses, but particularly on Purple Moor Grass (*Molinia caerulea*).

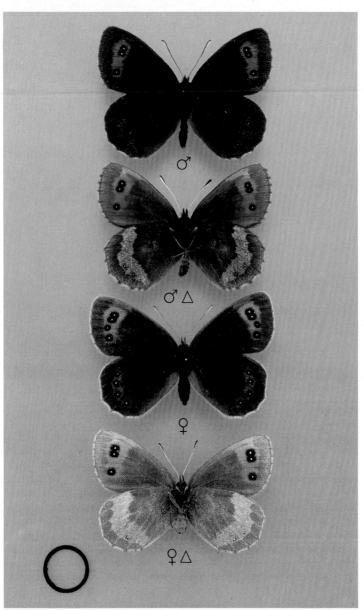

♂

♂ △

♀

♀ △

Scotch Argus

Ringlet at rest

Ringlet

Aphantopus hyperantus is widespread in Europe but absent from southern Spain, Italy and northern Scandinavia. In the British Isles it is widely distributed and locally common, although it does not occur in northern Scotland. In recent years, it has disappeared from many industrial regions and some populations have been affected by land drainage for agriculture. This is a very distinctive species, unlikely to be confused with any other European butterfly, but development of the characteristic ringed spots is very variable and they are sometimes absent altogether. It lives in damp situations in woodland clearings, hedgerows and meadows.

There is only one generation a year and butterflies are on the wing from June to August according to locality. They have a fairly feeble, fluttering flight, usually low down over the vegetation, and are often seen feeding at bramble (*Rubus*) blossoms. They also feed on various grasses such as Couch (*Agropyron repens*) and Meadow Grasses (*Poa*).

σ

σ △

♀

♀ △

Ringlet

Meadow Brown feeding

Meadow Brown

Maniola jurtina is one of the commonest and most widely distributed European butterflies, occurring almost everywhere except for the extreme north. It is widespread and common throughout the British Isles, with the exception of the Shetlands. It lives primarily in meadows and on the margins of agricultural land but also occurs in a wide range of grassland habitats from sea level up to 1800 metres. It will survive and breed in almost any situation where wild grasses are allowed to grow without cutting even on verges and waste ground in cities.

There is only one generation a year but the butterflies have a long flight period lasting from June to September under favourable conditions. They are active both in dull and sunny weather and have a fairly slow and fluttering flight, usually low over the vegetation. They often bask with their wings outspread in patches of weak sunlight.

The caterpillars feed on various grasses but particularly on species of Meadow Grass (*Poa*).

134

♂

♂ △

♀

♀ △

Meadow Brown

Gatekeepers mating

Gatekeeper

Pyronia tithonus, also known as the Hedge Brown, occurs widely in central and southern Europe and is locally common. It is absent from Scandinavia and southern Italy. In the British Isles it is common in southern England, lowland Wales and the south coast of Ireland, but is absent from Scotland and northern Ireland. It is most frequently encountered in hedgerows but is also found along the rough grassy margins of fields and in woodland rides and clearings.

There is a single generation each year and butterflies are on the wing from July to September according to locality and climate. They are very active in warm weather and have a rapid, dancing flight. Bramble (*Rubus*) blossom provides an attractive source of nectar.

The caterpillars feed on a wide range of grasses, including Meadow Grasses (*Poa*), Bents (*Agrostis*) and Fescues (*Festuca*).

The closely related Southern Gatekeeper (*Pyronia cecilia*), is restricted to southern Europe and lacks eye spots on both sides of the hindwing.

♂

♂ △

♀

♀ △

Gatekeeper

Large Heath

Large Heath

Coenonympha tullia is widely distributed in central and northern Europe. Its stronghold in the British Isles is in Scotland but it also occurs locally in northern England and Wales and in scattered localities throughout Ireland. It is a very variable butterfly and northern populations tend to have less well-developed eye spots on the wings than those occurring further south. This is a wetland species, living in a range of habitats from lowland marshes to moorland peat bogs and wet mountain meadows up to 2300 metres.

There is a single generation each year and butterflies are on the wing in June and July. They have a fairly slow and fluttering flight and rest frequently on the vegetation, although they are seldom attracted to flowers. In dull weather they hide close to the ground amongst vegetation.

The caterpillars usually feed on White Beak-sedge (*Rhynchospora alba*) and Cotton Grasses (*Eriophorum*) but will also eat Purple Moor Grass (*Molinia caerulea*).

♂

♂ △

♀

♀ △

Large Heath

Small Heath

Small Heath

Coenonympha pamphilus is a common little butterfly, found throughout Europe, except for the extreme north. It can be distinguished from several other small European species by the absence of distinct eye-spots on the underside of the hindwings. In the British Isles it is found virtually everywhere and is often abundant. It lives wherever its foodplants grow, in dry or well-drained habitats such as meadows, hedgerows, roadside verges, heathland, woodland glades, sand dunes and grassy mountain slopes up to 1800 metres.

There are usually two generations a year but in southern regions there may be more. Butterflies are on the wing from April to October, according to locality. They have a fairly lively, fluttering flight close to the ground and are active in both dull and sunny weather.

The caterpillars feed on various grasses, particularly Annual Meadow Grass (*Poa annua*), Bents (*Agrostis*) and Fescues (*Festuca*).

140

♂

♂ △

♀

♀ △

Small Heath

Speckled Wood at rest

Speckled Wood

Pararge aegeria occurs in all parts of Europe except for northern Scandinavia. Southern specimens have the upperside of the wings dappled with bright orange brown, whereas those from the north tend to be patterned with yellowish white. In the British Isles it is widespread in Ireland, Wales and southern and central England and occurs locally in northern England and parts of Scotland. This is one of the few butterflies that has extended its range in Britain in recent years. It lives in damp, shady habitats such as woodland rides and clearings and overgrown hedgerows.

There are usually two generations a year but in Scandinavia there is only one and in the extreme south of Europe there may be several. Butterflies are on the wing from March to October. They have a fairly slow, fluttering flight and are frequently seen basking in patches of sunlight or feeding at the blossoms of Bramble (*Rubus*).

The caterpillars feed on grasses such as Cocksfoot (*Dactylis glomerata*) and Couch (*Agropyron repens*).

♂

♂ △

♀

♀ △

Speckled Wood

Wall Brown basking

Wall Brown

Lasiommata megera is widespread throughout Europe except for northern Scandinavia. In the British Isles it is common and widely distributed in the south but becomes scarce further north and is absent from most parts of Scotland and the mountains of Wales. It lives in warm dry habitats such as hedgerows, roadside verges, heathland, downland, quarries, cliffs and open woodland.

There are two generations a year in the north and three in the south, with butterflies on the wing from March to September according to locality. They have a fairly rapid, fluttering flight but do not usually travel very far. As their name suggests, they are fond of basking on sunny walls but are also seen on sunbaked earth and in sheltered hollows on rocky ground.

The caterpillars feed on a wide range of grasses, including Cocksfoot (*Dactylis glomerata*), Yorkshire Fog (*Holcus lanatus*) and False Bromes (*Brachypodium*).

144

♂

♂ △

♀

♀ △

Wall Brown

Monarch feeding

Monarch

Danaus plexippus is a well-known American migratory species that occurs from time to time as a rare vagrant in the British Isles and parts of continental Europe. Recently there have been records of breeding colonies in the Malaga region of Spain, where milkweed (*Asclepias curassavica*), the foodplant of the caterpillar, is known to grow. These may have originated from the Canary Islands where the butterfly is established, having first arrived there in the late 19th century. The orange and black ringed caterpillars extract heart poisons from their foodplant. These remain in their bodies throughout their life and protect both caterpillars and butterflies from predators.

A closely related butterfly, the Plain Tiger (*Danaus chrysippus*) has also been recorded from southern Spain, although it is generally regarded as an African species. It can be distinguished from the Monarch by a lack of heavy black veining and the presence of conspicuous white markings on the forewings.

Monarch

Grizzled Skipper

Grizzled Skipper
Pyrgus malvae is widespread throughout Europe except for northern Scandinavia. In the British Isles it is confined to central and southern England and a few coastal localities in Wales. It lives in a wide range of habitats, from chalk downlands to woodland clearings and boggy meadows up to an altitude of 2000 metres.

In the north there is only one generation a year but further south a second brood occurs. The butterflies have a rapid, darting flight and are on the wing from April to August. Caterpillars feed on the foliage of Wild Strawberry (*Fragaria vesca*), Cinquefoil (*Potentilla*) and related plants.

The **Mallow Skipper,** *Carcharodus alceae,* is widespread in central and southern Europe but absent from Holland, Britain, north Germany and Scandinavia. There are from one to three broods a year, with butterflies on the wing from April to August according to locality and altitude. The caterpillars feed on Mallow (*Malva*) and Hollyhock (*Althea*).

Top: Mallow Skipper   Bottom: Grizzled Skipper

Large Chequered Skipper at rest, southern Dolomites

Dingy Skipper

Erynnis tages is a common and widespread species throughout Europe, except for the extreme north. It is widely distributed in the British Isles and is the only Skipper to occur in Ireland. It lives on chalk downland, roadside verges, railway embankments and other places where the food-plants grow.

There is one generation a year in the north and two in the south, with butterflies on the wing from May to August, according to locality. They have a rapid, whirring flight.

The caterpillars feed on Birdsfoot Trefoil (*Lotus corniculatus*) and other members of the pea family.

The **Large Chequered Skipper,** *Heteropterus morpheus*, is quite widely distributed in Europe but is absent from the British Isles, except for a very restricted locality in the Channel Islands. It lives in damp and marshy meadows. Butterflies are on the wing from June to August. The cater-pillars feed on various grasses.

Dingy Skipper   Large Chequered Skipper

Lulworth Skipper feeding, Lulworth Cove

Chequered Skipper

Carterocephalus palaemon occurs locally in north-eastern and central Europe. It recently became extinct in England but still survives in western Scotland. It lives in woodland rides and clearings and in rough grassland.

There is one generation a year and butterflies are on the wing from May to July. They are active in sunny weather, making short whirring flights.

The caterpillars feed on such grasses as False Brome (*Brachypodium*) and Purple Moor Grass (*Molinia caerulea*).

The **Lulworth Skipper,** *Thymelicus acteon,* is widely distributed in central and southern Europe but absent from the north. Its English stronghold is in Lulworth Cove although it also survives in a few other coastal localities in the south west. It lives on meadows, cliffs and mountain slopes.

There is one generation a year and butterflies are on the wing from May to September according to locality. They have a rapid, whirring flight.

The caterpillars feed on Tor Grass (*Brachypodium pinnatum*) and Bromes (*Bromus*).

♂

♂

♂ △

♂ △

♀

♀

♀ △

♀ △

Lulworth Skipper

Chequered Skipper

Small Skipper feeding

Essex Skipper

Thymelicus lineola is widely distributed throughout Europe, except for northern Scandinavia. In the British Isles it is most commonly found in south-eastern England, although it is also found in the south-west. It is absent from northern England, Wales, Scotland and Ireland. It lives on rough grassland in such places as hedgerows and roadside verges.

There is one generation a year and butterflies are on the wing from June till August. The caterpillars feed on various coarse grasses, such as False Brome (*Brachypodium*) and Cocksfoot (*Dactylis glomerata*).

The **Small Skipper**, *Thymelicus flavus*, has a similar distribution to the Essex Skipper in Europe but in the British Isles it is very common in most parts of southern and central England and in Wales. The two species are very similar in appearance and in habit and may often be found flying together. However, Essex Skippers can be recognised by the distinctive black tips to the undersides of their antennae.

Essex Skipper

Small Skipper

Silver-spotted Skipper at rest

Large Skipper

Ochlodes venata is widespread and common in Europe except for northern Scandinavia. In the British Isles it is common in lowland England and Wales and also occurs in south-west Scotland. It lives on rough grassland in such habitats as woodland clearings and waste land.

There is one generation in the north but further south there may be two or three generations. Butterflies are on the wing from June to August and have a strong, whirring flight.

The caterpillars feed on grasses such as Cocksfoot (*Dactylis glomerata*) and False Brome (*Brachypodium*).

The **Silver-spotted Skipper,** *Hesperia comma*, is widely distributed but local in Europe. In the British Isles it has become extremely scarce and only occurs in a few localities in southern England. It lives in dry meadows and on sunny hillsides, particularly on calcareous soils.

There is one generation a year and butterflies are on the wing in July and August. The caterpillars feed on Sheep's Fescue (*Festuca ovina*).

156

♂

♂

♂ △

♂ △

♀

♀

♀ △

♀ △

Silver-spotted Skipper

Large Skipper

INDEX

Other titles in this series:

Birds

Mediterranean Wild Flowers

Wild Flowers of Mountain and Moorland

Coastal Wild Flowers

Herbs and Medicinal Plants

Seashells and Seaweeds

Wild Flowers of Roadsides and Waste Places

Weeds

Trees

Mushrooms

Woodland Wild Flowers

David Carter works for the British Museum (Natural History), and is the author of *Butterflies* published by Pan in the Roger Phillips series.

The studio photographs in this book are by Frank Greenaway of the British Museum (Natural History) Photographic Unit, and the field shots were provided by Natural Science Photos and were the work of the following photographers: P A Bowman p. 2, Richard Revels p. 4, 20, 24, 34, 36, 38, 40, 50, 54, 56, 66, 68, 78, 104, 114, 126, 128, 130, 138; T Ruckstuhl p. 6, 14, 22, 30, 94, 100, 142; J Plant p. 8, 46; Nigel Charles p. 10, 16, 26, 32, 44, 52, 58, 60, 62, 64, 72, 74, 80, 82, 86, 98, 102, 106, 108, 110, 112, 116, 118, 120, 122, 124, 132, 134, 140, 144, 148, 150, 152, 154, 156; M Chinery p. 18, 92; Alan Barnes p. 28; P H and S L Ward p. 42, 76; P H Ward p. 48, 84; Simon Gardner p. 70, 90; G. Hannant p. 96; T A Moss p. 136; Michael Rose p. 146

ELM TREE BOOKS
Published by the Penguin Group
27 Wrights Lane, London W 8 5 T Z, England
Viking Penguin Inc., 40 West 23rd Street, New York, New York 10010, U S A
Penguin Books Australia Ltd, Ringwood, Victoria, Australia
Penguin Books Canada Ltd, 2801 John Street, Markham, Ontario, Canada L 3 R 1 B 4
Penguin Books (N Z) Ltd, 182–190 Wairau Road, Auckland 10, New Zealand
Penguin Books Ltd, Registered Offices: Harmondsworth, Middlesex, England
First published in Great Britain 1988 by Elm Tree Books
Copyright © 1988 by David Carter
Studio pictures Copyright © 1988 by the British Museum (Natural History)
ISBN 0-241-12160-4
ISBN 0-241-12159-0 Pbk
Printed and bound in Spain by Cayfosa Industria Gráfica, Barcelona